BOOK 3

NANCY CLANCY
Sees the Future

BOOK 3

NANCY CLANCY
Sees the Future

WRITTEN BY
Jane O'Connor

ILLUSTRATIONS BY
Robin Preiss Glasser

HARPER
An Imprint of HarperCollinsPublishers

To Kendall Messler for her invaluable help
—J.O'C.

For Bob: my past, present, and future
—R.P.G.

ISBN 978-0-06-208297-8

Typography by Jeanne L. Hogle
13 14 15 16 17   CG/RRDH   10 9 8 7 6 5 4 3 2 1
❖
First Edition

CONTENTS

CHAPTER 1

PAPER FORTUNE-TELLERS

"My turn to ask a question," Nancy said to Bree.

It was late afternoon. They were in their clubhouse telling fortunes. Fortune-telling was more fun to do in the dark. So they had taped together the sheets of the clubhouse. Now the only light came from

1

a flashlight. It kept flickering on and off because the battery was almost dead.

"Spooky," Bree said.

"Eerie," Nancy agreed.

Bree slipped her fingers into a paper fortune-teller. They had made so many that it looked like a flock of colorful birds had landed in the clubhouse.

In a low voice Bree whispered, "I will peer into the future now. Ask whatever you wish."

Nancy wanted to giggle. But giggling would wreck the eerie mood. So she forced

her lips to unsmile. Then she asked the same thing she'd asked a bunch of times before. "Will my mom give in and let me get pierced ears before my birthday?"

"Pick a color."

"Purple," Nancy told Bree, who began opening and closing the wings of the paper fortune-teller while she spelled out P-U-R-P-L-E.

Besides Nancy, only five third-grade girls didn't have pierced ears. And that was because they were scared to. Bree's ears had been pierced when she was a baby.

"Hey! Are you paying attention?" Bree said in her normal voice. "I said to pick a number."

"Seven," Nancy said. Once Bree had

opened and shut the fortune-teller seven times, Nancy got to select one of the flaps. "Mmmmm. The one with the star."

Bree cleared her throat. "The question is: Will you get your ears pierced before your birthday? The fortune-teller says . . ." Bree lifted up the paper flap and frowned. "It says, 'Unfortunately, no.'"

Nancy's heart sank. "It's hopeless."

Bree shrugged. "You know the answer doesn't mean anything. Fortune-telling is just pretend."

"Yes, I guess." Nancy reminded herself of all the times she'd gotten good answers to this very same

question. Paper fortune-tellers were fun.
But they weren't reliable. You couldn't
count on them to see the future.

After Bree went home, Nancy found her
mom and little sister in the kitchen. JoJo
was scribbling so hard in a coloring book
that the page was about to rip. Nancy's
mother was searching through the freezer.
"Guess I should have stopped at the super-
market after work." Her mom frowned.
"Well, gang, looks like it's macaroni and
cheese tonight, or—" She opened the pan-
try door to check there. "Or cheese and
macaroni."

Just then they all heard a car crunch
over the gravel in the driveway. JoJo
jumped up. "It's Daddy!"

"I bet he's bringing pizza." Nancy didn't know what made her say that. The words seemed to pop out of her mouth all on their own.

Not more than a second later, the kitchen door banged open. And *voilà!* Her father was holding a large flat cardboard box from the King's Crown. Nancy was surprised. In fact, she was more than surprised. She was astonished. "Dad, I just predicted you were bringing home

pizza. Didn't I, Mom?"

"Yup. She did."

Then Frenchy came racing down the stairs and ran in circles around Dad. Her tongue was hanging out and she was drooling like a maniac. That was because dogs had a superb sense of smell. Room 3D was learning about the five senses. Mr. Dudeny had explained that dogs could smell about a thousand times better than human beings.

Nancy helped her mom fix a salad. Then the Clancys all sat down in the dining room. There were candles and cloth napkins. It was one of Nancy's rules. Well, not

a rule, exactly. It just made dinnertime
fancy and civilized.

Nancy was on her second slice of pizza
when the phone rang in the kitchen.
"I have a feeling it's Grandma," Nancy

said. However, she didn't get up to answer the phone. That was one of her parents' rules. No calls during dinner.

After four rings, Grandma's voice came on. *"Hello, my darlings. Grandpa and I are hoping to come visit the weekend after next."*

"Goody!" JoJo said, and slurped up a long string of pizza cheese.

The message ended with Grandma making a loud kissing sound. *SMOOCH!*

"Didn't I predict it was Grandma calling?!"

"Hey. Do you have special powers we don't know about?"

"No, Dad. Of course I don't. . . . At least, I don't think I do."

During dessert the phone rang again.

"So who is it this time?" Nancy's dad wanted to know.

Nancy shut her eyes, but before there was time for the answer to float into her mind, she heard Bree's voice.

"My parents are going to see somebody's new baby at the hospital. So they're taking Freddy and me over to Annie's house. It's only for an hour. Want to come?"

"Oh, please? Can I?" Nancy begged her parents. Annie was seventeen and the most superb babysitter in the world. "I've never seen Annie's room, and Bree says it's spectacular."

Nancy predicted exactly what her mom would say next: "Do you have homework?"

Everybody in 3D had to write about a

special smell. Nancy's was on
the little cloth bag of dead
flowers that she kept in her
top drawer. It was called
sachet. You said it like this—
"sah-shay." It made her underwear smell
heavenly.

"I just have to put the finishing touches
on my paragraph." That sounded better
than saying she wasn't completely done.

Her mom looked uncertain.

"Mom, I'll finish it at Annie's. I promise.
In fact"—Nancy raised her right hand as if
she were on a witness stand—"I give you
my solemn oath."

Ooh la la! That sealed the deal.

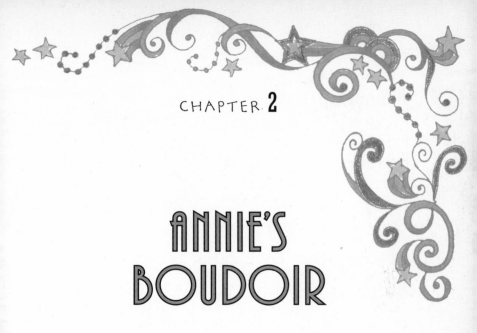

CHAPTER 2

ANNIE'S BOUDOIR

Fifteen minutes later, Bree's parents dropped off Nancy, Bree, and Bree's little brother at Annie's house. Freddy was already in his pj's. While Annie put on a video game for him in the den, Bree led Nancy down the hall.

"Ta-da!" Bree waited a beat before

flinging open the door to Annie's room.

"Nancy, can you believe how cool it is?"

Nancy entered and turned around slowly. She had never been in an actual teenager's room before. Everything was built-in—the desk, the bookcases, the dresser, even the bed, which was hidden inside a wall until Bree pulled a handle. Then, *voilà!* The bed appeared, like magic. The bedspread had orange and purple stripes. Annie's rug was orange and purple too. But it had polka dots, not stripes. Double ooh la la!

"I have dibs on the window seat," Bree said. She took out this week's list of spelling words from her backpack and began testing herself. The spelling test wasn't until Thursday. Not for three whole days. But

Bree had superb study skills. She always did schoolwork way ahead.

Watching Bree made Nancy remember her solemn oath. So Nancy put the finishing touches on her smell paragraph.

"Mrs. DeVine taught me how to make sachet. That's the French word for a little bag of dead flowers. You can also mix in pieces of cinnamon sticks and cloves to make the aroma even more delightful."

Done!

Bree was still spelling words out loud with her eyes closed. So Nancy took a tour of Annie's room, examining the glamorous teenage things in it. Best of all was Annie's earring tree. Hanging from its branches were tons of earrings—pearl drops, silver hoops, and clusters

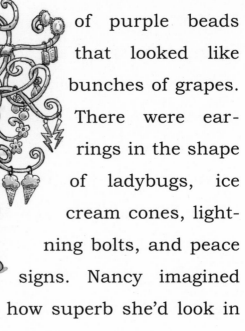

of purple beads that looked like bunches of grapes. There were earrings in the shape of ladybugs, ice cream cones, lightning bolts, and peace signs. Nancy imagined how superb she'd look in each and every pair.

At last Annie appeared.

"I love your boudoir," Nancy told her. "*Boudoir*" was French for bedroom. Nancy said it like this: "boo-dwah."

Then Annie, Nancy, and Bree all flopped down on the bed and looked through fashion magazines together.

"How come some of the pages here are ripped out?" Bree asked.

Annie pointed to her corkboard. The torn-out pages had photos of models with short hair. "Didn't I tell you? I'm getting my hair all cut off this Saturday."

"NO!" Bree and Nancy both screamed in horror. Annie's hair was perfect. It was black and shiny and so long she could sit on it. She let Nancy and Bree brush and style it any way they liked.

"It's for Locks of Love. They make wigs from real hair for kids getting treated for cancer. Often their hair falls out. My best friend and I are both doing it."

"Oh! What a thoughtful gesture!" Nancy exclaimed. Nancy's neighbor Mrs. DeVine always said that whenever Nancy did

something extra nice.

"And look!" Annie's purse was on the floor. She fished around for a pink box. Inside it was a pair of earrings. They looked like little chandeliers made of rhinestones. "I bought them today. They'll look great with short hair. Now all I have to do is decide which style I like best."

Nancy took another look at the photos on the corkboard. Then she closed her eyes partway, which made her eyelids flutter.

"Why are you making that goofy face?" Bree asked.

"Shh! I need complete quiet." Nancy

pressed her hands
on both sides of her
forehead. After
a moment she
said softly, "Annie,
you'll get the hairstyle
with bangs."

"What makes you so sure?" Bree asked.

Nancy opened her eyes. Bree was trying
on Annie's chandelier earrings.

"It's a feeling I have. A strong
feeling. I've been getting them
all night." Then Nancy told
Bree and Annie about the
pizza and the call from her
grandma.

Bree folded her arms
across her chest. "Don't be

silly. Those were lucky guesses."

It was irritating the way Bree sometimes sounded like Nancy's mother.

"Well, my—my dad thinks I may have special powers," Nancy stammered. That wasn't exactly true.

"Annie, tell her. Nobody can know stuff before it happens," Bree said.

Annie was sitting cross-legged on her bed. She shrugged. "I'm not sure. I've read about people who claim to have something called second sight. It's like a sixth sense. You know, like when you suddenly get a feeling that a long-lost friend is going to get in touch. And then it happens."

"See?" Nancy said.

Annie looked at Nancy and said slowly, "Well-l-l, I hate to bring this up. But remember when you both were *soooo* sure you knew exactly who I was going to fall in love with?"

"That was a long time ago," Nancy said, embarrassed. She and Bree had tried to fix Annie up with Nancy's guitar teacher. It hadn't worked out. "My powers are very new."

"No! You don't have powers!" Bree shook her head so hard, it made the earrings swing back and forth. "And there are only five senses." She ticked them off one by one on her fingers. "Taste, touch, smell, hearing, and sight. You can't have any more than that."

Nancy knew there was no point arguing. They went back to looking at Annie's fashion magazines. Nothing Nancy could say would change Bree's mind. Bree was super stubborn. There was a word for how stubborn Bree was: "obstinate."

On the way home from Annie's, Nancy and Bree didn't talk much. They weren't in a fight, exactly. It was more like a disagreement.

Later that night, Nancy picked out her outfit for the next day. Striped leggings. A purple hoodie. And her favorite shoes. They were glittery gold clogs and practically brand-new. But all of a sudden she started to have a funny feeling that it was going to rain tomorrow. As she thought about it, she became surer and surer. So Nancy put away the shoes and got out an old pair of ballet flats.

Then she placed a Magic Marker on her night table. It was a reminder for when she woke up. Every morning before school, she put a black dot on each earlobe for fake holes. It probably wasn't fooling anyone. Still, it made her feel better.

CHAPTER 3

PREDICTING RAIN

The next morning, Nancy and Bree walked to school together like always. Except it wasn't exactly like always. Why couldn't they just agree to disagree about Nancy's powers? That was what Mr. D suggested whenever two kids each thought the other was wrong.

At recess Bree ran off to the monkey bars. Nancy played four square with Lionel and a bunch of other kids. Then all of a sudden it began raining. At first there were just a few drops. But soon the rain started pounding down.

Everybody raced inside. They spent the rest of recess in the gym watching a movie about humpback whales. Every time it rained they watched either this movie or one about the different holidays that children around the world celebrated. It was very multicultural.

Lionel was sitting next to Nancy. He was snoring really loudly. When Mr. Dudeny came over and told him to cut it out, Lionel blinked and acted startled. "What? Where am I? Was I asleep?"

Nancy was bored too. She listened to the hard drops of rain ping-pinging against the windows. Then, like a slap, it came back to her. Last night she had predicted it would rain. That was why she had worn an old pair of shoes. The sun had been shining all morning until ten minutes ago. She clapped a hand over her mouth and let out a squeak.

Lionel heard it and turned to her. "Hey, are you going to regurgitate?" Nancy had

taught him that word. It meant throw up.

Nancy shook her head. She stared at Lionel. Lionel was her friend. He was a goofball, but he was also a talented magician. He took magic very seriously. She leaned in closer to him. "Promise you won't laugh if I tell you something weird? And promise to keep it a secret?"

"I promise."

"I think maybe I can see the future," Nancy whispered.

Lionel's eyes bugged out. "For real? That is so cool!"

On the way out of the gym, Lionel listened to all of Nancy's predictions that had come true. He kept nodding. Right before they got to their classroom, he took out a nickel and tossed it.

"Heads or tails?"

"Tails," Nancy said.

She called the toss correctly two more times before missing. Lionel looked astonished. "Oh, you have powers, all right!"

"I missed the last time," Nancy pointed out.

"That's because you're a beginner. Your powers will grow stronger!"

Hearing Lionel's words made Nancy swallow hard. So this *was* real! Her legs felt a little rubbery as she walked to her desk and sat down. And to think, only yesterday she had been an ordinary third grader.

CHAPTER 4

SENSE OR NONSENSE?

Mr. Dudeny collected everybody's smell paragraphs.

"Mine is about an undercover cop named Jimmy Aroma. He has a secret weapon—body odor," Lionel said. "He has killer BO."

"Eager to read it, dude," Mr. Dudeny said.

There was a big plastic model of a giant eyeball on his desk. The different parts came out like puzzle pieces. He explained what each part did. Afterward, for fun Mr. D passed around posters with pictures that played tricks on your eyes. "They are called optical illusions," Mr. D explained.

In one poster, Nancy sometimes saw a duck and sometimes a rabbit. In another, two dogs turned out to be exactly the same size even though one looked bigger than the other.

"Our eyes see things. They take in visual images," Mr. Dudeny said. "But something else makes sense of the things our eyes see. Anybody want to guess what that something is?"

Clara's hand went up halfway before

she pulled it down.

Mr. Dudeny had spotted her. "Yes, Clara?" He smiled an encouraging smile.

"Um . . . is it eyeglasses?"

"Eyeglasses do help make sense of what we see. But I was thinking of something besides eyeglasses."

Clara looked happy that at least her answer wasn't wrong.

"It's our brain!" Tamar shouted out.

"I don't remember calling on you, Tamar. But yes. Our brain interprets—it makes sense of—what our eyes see. And sometimes our brain gets fooled."

Now Bree's hand was raised. "But our eyes can only see what's right in front of them, nothing else."

"I'm not sure what you are asking, Bree."

"I want to know if there's such a thing as second sight, like a sixth sense."

"Do you mean, can people see the future?"

Bree nodded. Her desk was next to Nancy's. But she avoided Nancy's eyes.

"Ooh! Ooh! Mr. Dudeny!" Grace was nearly bouncing out of her seat. "My aunt went to a fortune-teller. The fortune-teller said my aunt was going to get rich. The next day she found a one-hundred-dollar bill in a parking lot."

"Okay, cool. But did your aunt ever win the lottery? Or end up marrying a millionaire?" Robert wanted to know.

"Um, not yet," Grace admitted. "Still, finding a hundred dollars . . . the very next day!"

Although several other hands were waving, it was almost lunchtime. So Mr. Dudeny had to table the discussion. That meant there was no more time to talk.

"We've been learning about the five senses." Mr. D paused. "Grace's aunt found a hundred dollars. Did the fortune-teller predict what would happen? No. I definitely don't think so." He looked around the class. "I'm sure all of us at some point have had a hunch—a sudden feeling about something—that came true. Is that the same as seeing the future? No." Mr. Dudeny wrote two words on the whiteboard: "coincidence" and "intuition." "By Friday, I'd like everyone to find out what these words mean and use them in a sentence."

"They won't be on the spelling test, will they?" Clara looked worried.

"No, they won't."

"Whew!" said Clara, right as the lunch bell rang.

A HUNCH AT LUNCH

When Nancy reached the end of the cafeteria line, she was happy to see Bree waving to her from their favorite table. It was under a poster of the four food groups. After opening their lunch bags, they decided to trade sandwiches.

"Um, look, can I ask you something?"

Bree said, handing over her tuna salad.

Uh-oh. Nancy had a hunch what the question would be.

"Do you still think you have powers? You heard what Mr. D said."

Nancy saw that Bree wanted her to say no. Nancy took a bite of Bree's cheese sandwich and thought about it. It was more than puzzling. It was perplexing. Lionel was certain she had powers. Yet if Nancy told Mr. D, he wouldn't believe it. And Mr. D was practically the most intelligent human being on the planet.

"I'm not sure," she finally said.

Clara and Tamar were setting down their trays. Then Grace appeared. "Come on, Nancy. Move over. There's room." After she squeezed onto the end of the bench, Grace stared at Nancy. "You know, those black dots on your ears look really dumb."

Nancy pretended not to hear.

Then Grace announced to everybody at the table, "Mr. D *is* wrong, by the way. W-R-O-N-G." That had been one of last week's spelling words.

"The fortune-teller my aunt went to definitely could see the future. She also said my aunt was going to travel to far-off places. And guess what? The next week a friend invited her to the North Pole."

"Grace, did you just make that up?" Clara said, shaking a little pile of Hershey's

Kisses onto the table. Clara was very fortunate. Her mother packed candy for her every day.

"I don't think there *are* trips to the North Pole," Tamar added.

"That's how much you know! My aunt says she'll take me to the fortune-teller if I want." Then Grace added, "It costs thirty dollars."

Thirty dollars! Nancy hadn't realized fortune-telling paid so well. A person could make a fortune telling fortunes!

All of a sudden, Bree stood up. "This is

a boring conversation. Fortune-tellers are fakes!" Then she picked up her tray and left. She didn't even bother taking any Hershey's Kisses.

CHAPTER 6

GOING PRO

After school, Lionel went home with Nancy. Tuesday was their weekly checkers game. The minute JoJo saw Lionel, she stopped blowing bubbles through the straw in her glass of milk.

"Show me magic!" she shouted.

"I don't have my wand with me."

47

"That's okay." JoJo handed him a straw.

So Lionel said, "Abracadabra," then waved the straw around and pulled a penny out of JoJo's ear.

JoJo shrieked with joy.

Lionel held the penny in his fist, then blew on it, and when his hand opened, the penny was gone.

JoJo hadn't seen it slip down Lionel's sleeve. "Do it again!"

Nancy's dad appeared just then. "Blow some bubbles, JoJo. Leave Nancy and Houdini alone."

"Who? Who's Deenee?" JoJo asked.

"I perform at birthday parties!" Lionel told Nancy and JoJo's dad as they headed upstairs. "My rates are very reasonable."

"Oh! That reminds me!" Nancy said to

Lionel. He was walking up the stairs back-ward with his eyes closed. "Grace's aunt, the one she told us about? It cost her thirty dollars to get her fortune told."

Lionel opened his eyes and whistled. "That's major money!"

In her room, Nancy got out the checkerboard. They set up the checkers and started to play. So far Lionel was ahead fourteen games to twelve. Nancy rubbed her hands together. "I have a feeling that today you're going to get clobbered."

Lionel was thinking about his next move. Then, his head shot up. "Like

those other feelings you got?"

Nancy looked up from the board and thought about it. "Yes! Just like them."

"See, what did I tell you? Your powers are growing. I think you should give some thought to going professional."

Even though Lionel was a total goofball, Nancy could tell he wasn't kidding. "Of course, you can't charge thirty dollars," he went on. "Not at first."

That made sense. "What price seems fair?" Nancy asked.

"Mmmmm. Maybe a quarter," Lionel said. "A quarter a question."

A quarter a question. Ooh la la! That had a nice ring. Nancy imagined a stack of quarters that kept growing taller and taller. She imagined all the earrings for pierced ears that she'd buy. By the time her birthday rolled around, she'd need an earring tree like Annie's.

"I could turn the clubhouse into a fortune-telling parlor."

"No. Do it at school during recess. Think of all the customers right there."

That was a superb point. Of course, not every third grader was going to pay Nancy to see the future. Nancy bet Bree wouldn't.

In fact, if Bree were here right now, she'd probably have lots of reasons why going into the fortune-telling business was a bad idea. But Bree wasn't here. She was at her piano lesson.

Nancy jumped up to get her art supplies. "I need a sign!" Nancy loved making signs. Ones in neon colors with fancy lettering.

They forgot about checkers and went to work.

The sign was super. It said:

Find out the future!

Only a quarter a question!

Lionel wanted to add "Satisfaction guaranteed!" at the bottom. Nancy didn't.

"That's too much pressure on me. I can't promise that every single thing I predict will come true."

Afterward, they painted Nancy's old Magic 8 Ball silver. Now it looked kind of like a crystal ball. The Magic 8 Ball had stopped working after JoJo dropped it and it cracked. But Nancy still remembered all the eerie answers that floated up. She'd use them tomorrow with her customers. *All signs point to yes. . . . It is unclear at this time. . . . Highly doubtful. . . . Ask again later.*

"All I need now is the right ensemble." Nancy explained to Lionel that ensemble meant her outfit. "I need a shawl for sure. One with fringe. A long, colorful skirt, maybe with ruffles, and gold dangly earrings."

CHAPTER 7

THE RIGHT ENSEMBLE

The fashion part of fortune-telling didn't interest Lionel. So Nancy waited until his mom came to pick him up. Then she raced next door to see Mrs. DeVine. Practically everything in Mrs. DeVine's closet was perfect for fortune-telling!

Later, Nancy tried on the clothes and

jewelry that Mrs. DeVine had let her borrow. She had to roll up the skirt around her waist, and the clip-on earrings pinched a lot. Still, gazing at herself in the mirror, Nancy had to admit it: She looked like a professional.

She called Lionel. "The crystal ball is almost dry and I've got my ensemble."

"Don't forget the sign," Lionel said. He was going to walk around the playground with it at the beginning of recess. "Wait a few minutes before you come out. Let the excitement build."

Ooh la la! Nancy would get to make a grand entrance!

Nancy had a hard time falling asleep that night. A funny feeling started bubbling up in her tummy. It wasn't one of her fortune-telling feelings. It was probably excitement. She hadn't told Bree about tomorrow. She hadn't discussed her new career with her parents, either. However, there was nothing wrong with using her powers to make money. Lionel made money from magic shows. Then a superb idea struck Nancy. The bubbly feeling went away. She wouldn't keep all of the fortune-telling money for herself. She'd give some away to a good cause. Just like Annie was doing with her hair for Locks of Love. That would make her parents proud.

They'd say, "Oh, Nancy. What a lovely gesture!"

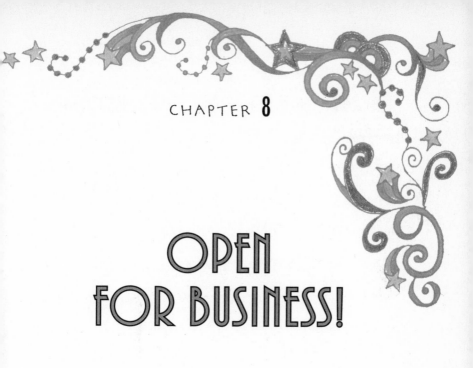

CHAPTER **8**

OPEN FOR BUSINESS!

T he next day, as soon as the bell for recess rang, Nancy grabbed her backpack and ducked into the girls' room. Lickety-split she changed into her ensemble and flung open the door to the hallway.

"Ow!" someone yelped.

The door had whacked someone!

It was Bree. Her hand was cupped over her nose. "Is it bleeding?" Bree asked.

Nancy nodded. Bree was trying hard not to cry. She hated the sight of blood, especially her own.

Nancy raced back into the girls' room for a wad of toilet paper. When she pushed open the door, slowly this time, Mr. Dudeny was in the hallway kneeling beside Bree. He had Kleenex for her.

"I'm so sorry!" Nancy said.

"What happened?" Mr. Dudeny asked.

Nancy told him. "It's all my fault! I feel terrible!" Tears pricked the corners of Nancy's eyes. "Mr. D, can I go with Bree to the nurse, please?"

"No, I'll take Bree. You go to recess. And next time, remember how heavy that door is and—"

"I know. Use caution," Nancy answered. Mr. Dudeny often said that to kids. It meant be careful.

Mr. D put an arm around Bree and led her down the hall.

Nancy was stunned. Why hadn't her powers warned her that an accident was going to happen?

On the playground, Lionel was parading around with the sign. "What's in *your* future? Just ask Nancy!" he shouted over and over.

Nancy made a grand entrance, though her heart wasn't really in it. She hoped Bree's nose had

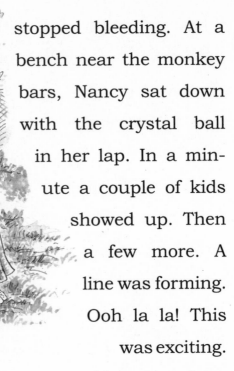

stopped bleeding. At a bench near the monkey bars, Nancy sat down with the crystal ball in her lap. In a minute a couple of kids showed up. Then a few more. A line was forming. Ooh la la! This was exciting.

All these people were seeking the advice of a professional—Nancy Clancy!

For now Nancy decided to put Bree out of her mind. She needed to concentrate on her powers. She closed her eyes halfway and smiled in a way that she hoped looked mysterious. "I am ready now."

Then Grace barged to the front of the line and tried to wreck everything.

"No fair! Nancy got this idea from me! After she heard about my aunt!"

"I did not," Nancy said with dignity. "I happen to have powers."

"Oh, right!" Grace's arms were folded across her chest. "Be—besides," she stammered angrily, "you need a license to tell

fortunes! It's the law!"

Nancy was pretty sure Grace was making that up. Then Lionel appeared and told Grace to get to the back of the line. Instead, Grace stomped off. "If you want to waste your money, go ahead!" Grace told all the kids in line.

Joel was up first. He handed over a quarter and asked, "Will I be an astronaut when I grow up?"

Nancy didn't need to wait for her powers to kick in. Every Halloween, Joel went as an astronaut. Next summer he was going to space camp. And he'd read every book in the library about the solar system. Nancy rubbed the crystal ball and made her

eyelids flutter. "All signs point to yes."

Olivia was next. She asked, "Will my mom have a girl?"

The baby was going to be born soon. Nancy knew that Olivia wanted a little sister. "It is almost certain!" she said.

The line grew longer. The questions got harder.

Robert wanted to know which team would win the Super Bowl. Nola wanted to know what play the third grade was going to put on. The teachers were keeping it a secret until next week.

Both times Nancy scrunched her eyes shut and concentrated on letting her powers go to work. But no answers floated into her mind. She ended up saying, "It's not clear at this time."

Robert and Nola looked disappointed, which made Nancy feel bad. But they paid anyway. After that Nancy told customers to stick to yes-or-no questions. "My powers work better that way," she explained.

"Okay." Nola fished out another quarter from her pocket. "Will I get to go to Disney World over spring break?"

"Yes," Nancy said after a moment. But it was just a guess. Not even a hunch. Nola let out a happy squeal. Somehow that made Nancy feel even worse.

What was going on? Her powers seemed to have deserted her. It was very noisy on the playground. Maybe that was the problem. In the class unit on the five senses, Nancy had learned about sound waves. It was very possible that all the sound waves

bouncing around were getting in the way of the waves that were trying to travel from the future.

Nancy was relieved when the line came to an end. Clara was the last person in it.

"Will I get everything right on the spelling test tomorrow?" Clara asked.

Without thinking, Nancy blurted out, "It is highly doubtful."

"Rats!" Clara said.

Right away Nancy wished she could take back the words. Nancy didn't want to take Clara's money. Clara insisted.

"I figured that'd be the answer." Clara shrugged. "It's not your fault what the future holds."

CHAPTER 9

CHANGING THE FUTURE

Bree wasn't in the classroom when Nancy returned from recess.

"Is Bree still at the nurse's?" she asked Mr. Dudeny. Nancy was back in her normal clothes now. The earrings had pinched so hard, they left red marks.

"No. The nosebleed stopped right away.

71

However, her head was hurting a little. So her mother came and took her home."

Nancy's hands flew to her heart. "I feel so guilty! I'm to blame for this!"

"It wasn't a serious accident," Mr. Dudeny assured her. He let Nancy call Bree on his cell phone. She was eating ice cream and sounded fine.

"*Merci* a million times, Mr. D," Nancy said. "Hearing Bree's voice was such a relief!"

Still, during creative writing, Nancy had trouble working on a new adventure for Lucette Fromage. She was a nine-year-old detective Nancy had made up.

Nancy's mind kept wandering. If only there was a way to make the past un-happen . . . like rewinding a video.

Everything from today would run back-
ward at top speed until Nancy was
changing in the girls' room before recess.
After the stop button was pushed and
the action started up again, Nancy would
open the bathroom door—very slowly the
first time. Nancy would also take back

her answer to Clara's question about the spelling test.

Nancy watched Clara at her desk. She was twirling her pencil and staring into space. Suddenly inspiration struck. That meant Nancy was getting a good idea. Maybe even a superb one.

"Can you bike over to my house this afternoon?" she asked Clara later. "I want to tutor you in spelling. Tutoring is like teaching, only in private. We'll go over the words until you can even spell them backward."

Clara giggled. Then she shrugged. "It won't do any good. Remember what you predicted?"

"I'm really sorry about that."

"Why? You can't help what you saw." Clara shrugged again. "I always goof up spelling words."

"But the test hasn't happened yet. There's time to change the future."

Clara looked uncertain. "You really think it works that way?"

Nancy nodded. "All signs point to yes."

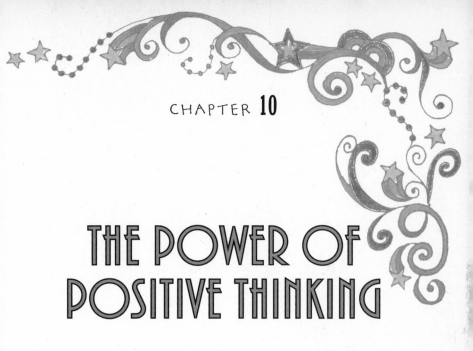

CHAPTER 10

THE POWER OF POSITIVE THINKING

Clara arrived as Nancy was setting up the stand on her old blackboard. It belonged to JoJo now. JoJo agreed to let Nancy use it on one condition.

"I get to play school too," she said.

"I told you. We're not playing school.

77

It's serious work."

"JoJo can stay. I don't mind," Clara said. She thought JoJo was cute.

Nancy wrote out all the spelling words. They were five-sense words all ending in "-ing," except the word of the week. That was "fragrant."

seeing
tasting
hearing
eating
feeling
smelling
sniffing
touching
peering
*fragrant

First Nancy had Clara spell the words while looking at them on the blackboard. "Now close your eyes. I'll say each word and you spell it back to me."

Clara wanted to skip the word of the week. "It's too hard. I'll never remember it."

"Clara, you have to have a positive attitude," Nancy said. "But we can leave 'fragrant' for the very end."

Pretty soon Clara could spell nearly all the words. But she kept mixing up "hearing" and "peering." She spelled them "heering" and "pearing."

"Remember Mr. D's trick? 'Hearing' has 'ear' in it." Nancy circled the "ear" part with her chalk. It made her feel very professional.

Clara nodded. "Still, I don't see why

'peering' isn't spelled like 'hearing.' They rhyme."

Clara had a point.

"It's snack time now," JoJo interrupted.

"No, it isn't," Nancy said.

"JoJo, why don't you be in charge of snacks?" Clara suggested.

JoJo clapped her hands. "I'm snack leader! Goody!" She skipped out of the room.

"Smart move!" Nancy high-fived Clara. Then she went back to the spelling list. She peered at the word "peering."

"Hey! I thought of a trick." Nancy giggled. "All you have to do is remember that 'peering' has 'pee' in it." Nancy drew a chalk circle around the letters. Clara giggled too. She closed her eyes. "P-E-E," Clara began. She spelled "peering" correctly three times.

They were working on "fragrant" when JoJo reappeared with a plate of cookies and apple slices. At the same time, the bell rang on the Top-Secret Special Delivery mailbox.

Nancy opened her window and pulled in the basket. It hung from a rope strung between her window and Bree's.

"Before you came, I sent a message to Bree asking

if she wanted company," Nancy explained to Clara as she unfolded the message. "Oh, good. Bree says to come over now."

They brought the cookies with them.

Bree was in her parents' bedroom. She was lying on a chaise. That is a kind of

armchair that stretches way out in front. You say it like this: "shays."

Bree had a little plastic bag with ice pressed against her face. "Look!" she said, and lowered the plastic bag.

Bree had a black eye! Except it wasn't black. It was purplish.

"Oh, *chérie!* I'm so sorry! Does it hurt?"

"No. It feels fine. I have to keep ice on it so it doesn't swell up."

"It's a pretty color," Clara said.

Nancy agreed. "It's the same shade as that eye shadow Annie has. Purple Passion."

While they were eating the cookies, Clara told Bree about Nancy helping her for the spelling test. "So the future won't come true," Clara explained.

Nancy's cookie dried up in her mouth.

Bree looked perplexed. "What?"

"Bree! You were there when Nancy was telling fortunes, remember?" Then Clara smacked her forehead. "Silly me! I forgot. You *weren't* there. It was at recess."

Nancy stood up. "Um, Clara, maybe we should let Bree rest some more."

"No. Come on. I want to hear." The bag of ice covered half of Bree's face, which made it hard for Nancy to tell what Bree was thinking.

So Clara filled Bree in. At the end, she said, "I better get going now. I have to bike home before dark or my mom'll kill me." Clara grabbed a cookie for the road.

When it was just the two of them, Bree asked, "How much money did you make?"

"A dollar seventy-five. Are you mad?"

"No. It's not fair to be mad. I'm not the boss of you." Bree split the last cookie with Nancy. "Are you going to tell fortunes again tomorrow?"

Nancy sank down on the end of the chaise. "I don't think so." She paused.

"No. I'm not." Bree was her best friend. She could tell her anything. "I was just guessing answers. I think my powers ran out."

"You mean like a flashlight battery?"

"Yes, Bree. Just like that. Otherwise I wouldn't have bonked you in the face."

"But you didn't know I was on the other side of the door. It was just an accident."

Nancy sighed. "Exactly. My powers should have seen the accident coming and warned me. And they didn't."

Right at that moment, Bree's mom popped her head in. "Sorry, ladies. It's time for Nancy to go home. And Bree, keep the ice pack on!"

UNPOWERED

The next morning, Bree was back in school but Clara was out sick. That was a shame. Clara was going to miss the spelling test. Last night Nancy had called to tutor her on "fragrant." Nancy couldn't think of any trick to learn it. She just made Clara repeat the letters over and over. By the time they hung up, Clara had "fragrant" down cold.

Nancy, however, got it wrong on the test. She forgot the second *r*. Nancy hadn't predicted she'd get "fragrant" wrong. She also hadn't predicted it would rain. Otherwise she wouldn't have worn her gold clogs. It looked like her powers were gone for good. *Au revoir.*

On the screen in the gym, a bunch of kids in China were flying kites that looked like dragons. Nancy didn't mind being stuck indoors or sitting through the movie about foreign children. Because there was no recess, she didn't have to make up excuses about why she wasn't telling fortunes.

At the end of the day Mr. Dudeny reminded everybody about the words "intuition" and "coincidence." "Dudes, find out what they mean and we'll discuss them tomorrow."

As soon as Nancy got home, she tried to look up both words in her dictionary. Neither word was there. So Nancy went downstairs to the living room and looked up the definitions in the big dictionary. Oh, how she adored long words—and "definition" was such a superb one. It was a

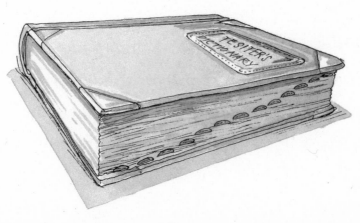

long word that explained what other long words, and short ones, too, meant.

Frenchy had been sleeping in her doggy bed. Now she jumped on the couch and curled up next to Nancy. "Coincidence" came before "intuition," so Nancy looked that up first.

A "coincidence" meant something surprising and unusual that happened just by chance. Bree's parents both had the same birthday. That counted as a coincidence. Was it fair, Nancy wondered, for her to use that example in class tomorrow? The coincidence belonged to Bree, after all. On the other hand, two people could think of the same example. Maybe that counted as a coincidence too!

"Intuition" meant a good guess. Long ago, when the Clancys had gone to an animal shelter in town, Nancy's intuition had told her Frenchy was the right puppy to bring home.

The phone in the kitchen started ringing.

Nancy heard her mom say, "Oh, hi! Yes, sure I've got a minute."

After that her mom said, "She was doing what?"

And after that she said, "No! I had no idea."

Nancy wished she could hear the other side of the conversation. She bet JoJo had been bad again at preschool. Last week JoJo's teacher had called because JoJo kept hogging all the blocks in the blocks corner.

"Well, I'm very sorry about this. I'm going to discuss this with her right now!"

Ooh, it looked like JoJo was really in for it.

"Nancy!" her mom called loudly. "Nancy! Where are you?"

Say what?

"In here," Nancy answered in a small

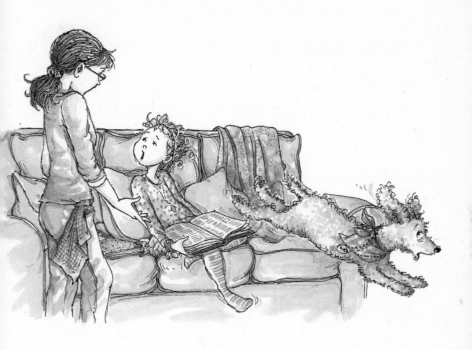

voice. "Doing homework."

Her mom strode into the living room. Frenchy jumped off the couch and skittered upstairs. Frenchy could always smell trouble.

"Clara's mother just called," Nancy's mom said. "It seems we have a little situation here."

A situation? That was never good.

"Yesterday . . . were children paying you to tell their fortunes?"

"Um. Yes."

"And did you tell Clara that she wasn't going to do well on a spelling test?"

"Not exactly. I said it was highly doubtful. But then I tutored her."

Her mom just kept shaking her head. "Well, Clara stayed home today pretending to be sick. Later her mother found out the real reason. Clara didn't want to take the spelling test."

"But she knew all the words. Even 'fragrant.' I spent ages tutoring her," Nancy repeated, hoping her mom might say what a thoughtful gesture that was.

"Clara woke up with a tummy ache. She

was nervous because of your prediction."

Nancy sighed. "I explained how it didn't have to come true, how we could change the future." She shut the big dictionary. "If you ask me, Clara needs to get a more positive attitude."

"No. That is not the prob—" Nancy's mom rubbed her forehead. She blinked and looked confused. "Hold on a minute. Are you saying that you honestly believe you can see the future?"

Nancy nodded. "I could for a while. I had powers. Remember the pizza and the call from Grandma? I said both were going to happen and they did."

"Oh, honey. Those were hunches. Good guesses."

"You mean intuition."

"Exactly. Think how often Dad brings home pizza. And how many nights does the phone ring during dinner and it's Grandma?"

"Well, w-well—I predicted rain the next day, and it did."

"Which day? Tuesday?"

Nancy nodded.

"The Weather Channel said there'd be rain."

Nancy spread out her hands. "But did I know that? No!"

"Yes, as a matter of fact, you did. When you came home from Annie's, you sat in the living room with Dad and me. The Weather Channel was on. You described Annie's earring tree in great detail and asked if I'd reconsider letting you get your ears pierced. Remember?"

Hmmmm. Perhaps Nancy did recall that part.

"The weather report was on the whole time. Even though you weren't paying attention," her mom went on, "it must have stuck in the back of your mind."

"Really?" Nancy sat back and pondered. Pondering meant her brain was thinking extra hard. So . . . her ears had heard things while her brain was half switched off? Did that mean she'd never had powers? Then

Nancy remembered the coin toss with Lionel. Ha! Her mother couldn't explain that away. "Mom, I called a coin toss right three times in a row. Are you saying that was only a coincidence?"

"No. It was luck. Odds. Every time a coin is tossed, there's a fifty percent chance it'll come up what you call."

Room 3D hadn't gotten to "percent" yet. "What?" Nancy asked.

Her mom reached into a pocket of her jeans. She got out a nickel and tossed it up. "Heads or tails?"

Lionel's nickel had worked much better than her mother's nickel. This time, Nancy missed the coin toss two out of three times.

"Sweetie, you can't see the future.

Nobody can." Her mother put an arm around Nancy. "All you can do is work hard so there's a better chance of making things turn out the way you want. That's what you were doing when you helped Clara."

Nancy leaned her head against her mother's shoulder. Her mother always smelled a little like warm bread. It wasn't perfume. It was a special mom scent.

"Do you understand what I'm saying, Nancy?"

"Yes. Mr. Dudeny said the same thing." Nancy pondered some more and came to a conclusion. "It's probably better that my powers weren't real." It had been exciting. It made her feel special. But what if she'd started seeing scary stuff that was going to happen? Nancy imagined herself running around trying to warn people about earthquakes or alien invasions. No. Not alien invasions. They weren't real either.

Her mom smiled at her. She didn't look angry anymore. Then she said, "So tomorrow, I want you to return the money to everyone."

Nancy felt like she'd been zapped in the back with a joy buzzer. "No! Please don't make me do that! Can't I just give the money to a good cause? I was going to anyway." Then Nancy added, "Well, not all of it. But some."

Her mom didn't answer right away.

"Please, Mom. Please," Nancy pleaded. "What'll I say? That I'm a big fake? Grace will never let me live it down!"

Her mom seemed to be pondering now. Finally she stood up and said, "Honey, you're not a little girl anymore. You're old enough to decide for yourself what to say."

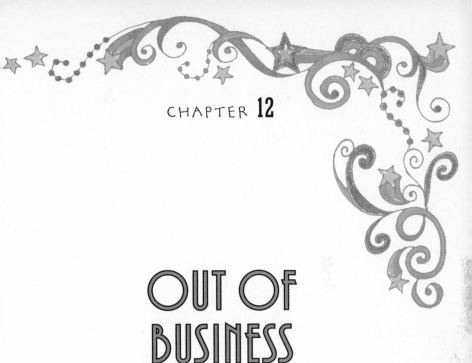

CHAPTER 12

OUT OF
BUSINESS

The next morning, Nancy and Bree met up at the corner. Bree was wearing sunglasses to protect her black eye and looked *très* glamorous. Nancy had a bunch of envelopes in her backpack— with the money she was giving back—as

107

well as a perfect excuse. She had written a note that said:

It has come to my attention that no one is permitted to make money on school property. So I am returning your money. I have also decided to quit the fortune-telling business for good.

Yours truly,

Nancy Clancy

"You were right all along," Nancy admitted to Bree as they walked to school. "I never had powers. Nobody does. All the stuff that I thought was seeing the future was only good guessing."

Bree stopped on the sidewalk. "Okay . . . I have to admit something to you too." Bree scrunched up her face. "I didn't want you to have powers. . . . I was jealous. You had something special that I didn't."

"So you believed in my powers!"

"A little. I wasn't sure. It also made you too different from me. That made me feel funny. I like us both just being regular girls."

Yes, Nancy could understand that. "My fortune-telling ensemble sure was lovely. I wish you had seen it. I wore a long, ruffly skirt of Mrs. DeVine's and a shawl and these big clip-on gold earrings."

At school Mr. Dudeny asked everyone to wait outside the classroom for a minute. "Clara is almost done taking the spelling test that she missed."

When the door opened again, Clara

was hopping around her desk doing a little victory dance.

"I nailed it!" She came over and hugged Nancy. "I remembered 'ear' in 'hearing'"—she lowered her voice—"and 'pee' in 'peering.' My mom says that seeing the future is crazy talk but that you're right about having a positive attitude."

Nancy decided to hand out the envelopes at recess. Grace was busy jumping rope, double Dutch, with girls from one of the other third-grade classes.

First Nancy went up to Joel. Joel was kneeling in the dirt. "Eight, seven, six . . ." he counted down. Nancy waited for his

110

Lego spaceship to blast off.

"Joel, I have something for you."

Joel wasn't paying attention. "This is Mission Control. The third-stage rockets have fired. You are leaving Earth's atmosphere."

Nancy was about to leave the envelope on the ground, where he'd be sure to see it. Then something really weird happened. Nancy's hands tore open the envelope and took out the quarter. Her finger tapped Joel on the back, and when he spun around, she held out the quarter. "I shouldn't have taken money from you. I can't see the future."

Joel looked irritated at being interrupted. "I never really thought you could." He pocketed the quarter. Then he went back to zooming his spaceship around and around.

Nancy told the truth to everybody. It turned out not to be a big deal. Lionel was the most disappointed. "Your career was just getting started!"

As soon as she got home, Nancy told her mother about returning the money. "Nobody was mad. And Grace doesn't even know. I had this great excuse made up, but something stopped me from fibbing. Mom, it was like this invisible force came out of nowhere and took possession of me! It forced me to tell the truth."

Her mom smiled and kissed the top of Nancy's head. "I know about that kind of invisible force. . . . It's called your conscience."

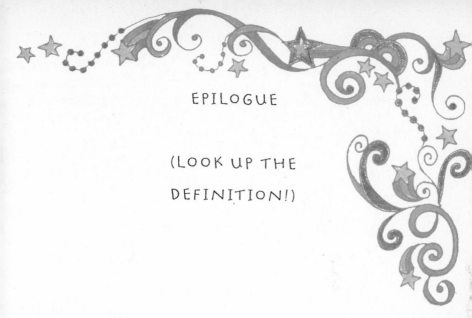

EPILOGUE

(LOOK UP THE
DEFINITION!)

On Saturday, Bree and Nancy ran into Annie at Belle's Fashion Boutique. Her hair was very short.

"It's most becoming," Nancy said to be polite. She could tell Bree didn't like Annie's haircut either.

"Up till when I sat down in the chair at the salon, I thought I was going to get the hairstyle with bangs, the one Nancy predicted," Annie said. "Then I changed my mind. This is called the Chop."

It didn't surprise Nancy that another one of her predictions turned out to be wrong. However, as they waved good-bye to Annie, Nancy told Bree, "I can make

one prediction that I absolutely, positively know will come true."

They had been looking through the jewelry case. Bree wanted to know which earrings Nancy liked best, and Bree would buy them for her birthday. Now suddenly, an "Oh no, not the powers again!" look came over Bree's face.

Then Nancy said, "I can predict right now what I'm going to be next Halloween."

Bree giggled. "I bet I can predict that too."

At the same time they both said, "A fortune-teller!"

About the Author

JANE O'CONNOR is truly a native New Yorker. She was born and raised on the glamorous Upper West Side and, after graduating from Smith College, returned to the metropolis (that's fancy for city) to begin a career in publishing. Currently Jane works as an editor for Penguin Books for Young Readers.

Jane has written more than sixty books for children, including the bestselling Fancy Nancy books, seven of which were #1 *New York Times* bestsellers.

Jane is married to Jim O'Connor. They have two grown sons and a rambunctious canine (that's fancy for naughty dog) named Arrow.

About the Illustrator

ROBIN PREISS GLASSER, a former professional ballet dancer, has illustrated more than fifty children's picture books, including the *New York Times* bestselling Fancy Nancy series, written by Jane O'Connor. Robin lives in San Juan Capistrano, California, with her husband, Bob. She has two grown children, Sasha and Ben, and a dog, Boo, who looks exactly like Nancy's dog, Frenchy!

A CHAPTER BOOK SERIES STARRING EVERYONE'S FAVORITE FANCY GIRL